STREET LOVE

Walter Dean Myers

Amistad
HarperTempest
An Imprint of HarperCollinsPublishers

Amistad and HarperTempest are imprints of HarperCollins
Publishers.

Street Love
www.harperteen.com
      Library of Congress Cataloging-in-Publication Data
Myers, Walter Dean, date
    Street love / Walter Dean Myers. — 1st ed.
      p.   cm.
    Summary: In this Harlem story told in free verse,
seventeen-year-old Damien takes a bold step to ensure that
he and his new love will not be separated.
    ISBN-10: 0-06-028079-4 (trade)
    ISBN-13: 978-0-06-028079-6 (trade)
    ISBN-10: 0-06-028080-8 (lib. bdg.)
    ISBN-13: 978-0-06-028080-2 (lib. bdg.)
    1. African Americans—Juvenile fiction. [1. African
Americans—Fiction. 2. Love—Fiction. 3. Harlem (New York,
N.Y.)—Fiction.] I. Title.
PZ7.M992Str 2006   2006002457
[Fic]—dc22   CIP
                                                             AC

Typography by R. Hult
1 2 3 4 5 6 7 8 9 10

First Edition

To Constance

HARLEM

Autumn in Harlem.
Fume-choked leaves, already
Yellowed, crack in the late September
Breeze. Weeds, city tough, city brittle,
Push defiantly along the concrete edges
Of Malcolm X Boulevard. On 137th Street
A toothless sidewalk vendor neatly stacks
His dark knit caps beside the plastic cell
Phone covers. Shadows indistinct in August heat
Now deepen and grow long across
The wide streets. Homeless men sniff the air and
Know that somewhere the Hawk stirs.
Harlem is not an easy place
To grow old, and so the young
Are everywhere,
Pouring from the buses, city dancing
To the rhythms of the street,
City dancing to the frantic spin of life
In the fast lane.

The *HERO*

Here we see a busy school yard
Black, brown, and tan forms
Painting the illusion of music
With their bodies, ball-dancing between the
White lines of the court.
Young Damien Battle, comfortable in stride and
    gesture
Wearing his seventeen years easily around broad
Shoulders, saunters at the unhurried pace of
Hero knowing that the space that
Opens before him is his due.
Beside him, perhaps a half step
Behind, his friend Kevin chatters easily.
They are young and proud and Black
For them life is a ripe orange
Succulent and sweet, ready to be devoured
And here are Sledge and Chico
Rivals from the other side of the Avenue

Their tribe is the more familiar
We have seen them on every corner
Of every city in America. They make us walk
Faster. They make us think of locked doors.
Of differences we would like to deny.
Do Sledge's eyes meet Damien's?
Does he sneer as he spins his basketball
On one brown finger as if it was the World?
Does he speak?
Does he speak?
We listen as Sledge's mocking voice
Lifts itself above the background clatter

DAMIEN
and SLEDGE

"Yo, Chico, check it out.
Yo, Chico,
There goes Damien, sliding and gliding
Past the court. Just strolling
And rolling his eyes
Away from the action
So we can't get the satisfaction
Of him peeping our dazzle."

"Peeping your dazzle?" Damien replies,
White toothing all over Sledge.
"I thought I was scoping the
Frazzled chumdom of a downtown clown."

"My game is my name," Sledge replies.
"Call it if you want some."

Damien shakes his head

"Yo, Sledge, if talk was walk my man you would be
Halfway round the world. You're confusing
    game with
Lame and Ball with stall. But at the end of the
Day your rap is weaker than your play."

Sledge comes chest to chest with Damien.
His eyes are slits that carve into the flesh.

"Yo, Damien, Listen up, man
Your mouth is shouting and your lips are pouting
Like you're somebody's girlfriend
Running off to double latteville
'Cause you know you ain't got the heart
To start no get down with me."

Damien scoped the scene and weighed it
Sledge's crew was throwing signs
And gritting teeth
They wore their colors but Damien didn't
Know what was beneath those jackets

"Yo, Sledge, we'll get it straight one day,"
Damien said. "Just the two of us.
Not now, not here, but we'll know when
We got to do what it looks like we got to do."

A brief conversation, hard looks in the air
Damien walks away and Sledge stares.
No big thing.
No big thing.
Just two seventeen-year-olds
Checking out a manhood jam.
Damien and Kevin make their way out
Breathing easier as they start up to Sugar Hill
The late summer shadows accentuate the edges
Of the hood, define it in shape and size
Yes, and darkness
The shadows on the corner shift as they walk by
Sharp eyes weigh their pockets from the distance
Heavy sisters weighing down the white brick
Stoops watch the passing scene
As they have for a hundred years

KEVIN *and* DAMIEN

"Yo, Damien, how you read Sledge?
Is he just about being a fool
Or do you think that his brain
Is twisted enough to find something
Cool in that lip and drip world he's sliming
In?"

"Sniff the hood, my man," Damien said. "The bad
    with the
Good. Some guys are banking on their reach
Going for the stars, scoping on the great,
Some see they can't reach and all they got is hate
To lift them from misery of the day and there's
Nothing you can say if their eyes don't see
The prize the way you do. That's the hood, bro,
That's the way it flows and it don't make
No never mind if you find yourself

Off the glory ride and slipping with the tide
Like Sledge. Hate is what the man
Got and if it's not boss he's got to toss it
Anyway. This is a concrete Apple."

"Damien, so are you saying
You're ready to fly?
Cop some getaway like all the other sleek
Birds winging through distant trees with just
An occasional peek
Now and then and a slanted rap about
Old school memories?"

"Who knows, man?" Damien said, checking out
    a tall
Brother working on his gangster lean.
"You're talking about
What tomorrow will bring, and what tune the
    hood will
Sing. You're talking and I'm listening, but
There's no clear message glistening on my
Horizon."

"Yo, you're sliding deep but my brain is still
Creeping on the surface," Kevin said. "Break it on
Down or push it on. It don't make no never mind."

"My moms was asking me to do the same layout
But that's all played out when you don't
Know which way the wind is blowing
Or which way you're supposed to be going
My folks are laying lines on me like
They've written out the part and all
I got to do is get to a place called Start
And follow the road to fame and glory—
A PhD in mucho buckology
Two point five kids and a quick apology
To the starving folks in East Ain'tGotNothingVille
While I look down from Sugar Hill and tell
Myself how phat my program is."

"Sounds righteous, my brother,
Best listen to your mother
Now what I need is for you to feed
Me the name of the female lead

Is the right chick a light chick?
Some straight-haired honey
With a little money and a skinny little nose
Pointing away from her toes?
Or could it really be a girl with some kink to
    her curl?
A midnight mama with some snap and some sway
Like that treetop sister 'cross the way
Walking like the Queen of the Avenue
Could she interest a lord like you?"

Damien looked, he had seen her before
He knew her name, but not much more

"Yeah, I see her," he said. "She's the quiet kind
I don't know her game, or what's in her mind."

"And if you found her in your net," Kevin asked,
"What then? Would you throw her back?
Or could she be a midday snack?"

"Yo, Kevin, you know I have a plan
And you know I have Roxanne. I'm not into

Fast foods or the easy line
Although I have to admit the lady's
Fine as she needs to be but can
She satisfy the brain or the heart
I don't know."

"Damien, Main Man, that girl might not satisfy
Your brain or your heart," Kevin said. "But, Lord
     knows,
There are parts of me that find her
Delightful. We should catch
Her and offer her our sweet company."

"No," Damien said. "She might be light, I haven't
Spoken more than a word or two with her. But
She walks darkly, as if her mind weighs down
Her steps.
When we've spoken it was just puffs of air
Syllables that weren't there
When we said them and left nothing
On the memory.
I don't know what she thinks
Of if she thinks of anything so profound

That it would interest me, and I'm not a snob
But she's a depth I have not sounded.
I wonder what a movie of her life would be
What images come to fill the screens
Of her mind?"

The BEAUTY

My head is filled with images as I stumble,
Heavy-footed through this endless day.
Terrible images of my mother's face
Twisted in disbelief, her body trembling
As the realization that her life was finished
Washed over her.
Her mouth was open but all that I could
Hear was the wailing of her soul
As they hustled her from the chaos of the
    courtroom
Into the chaos of the foreverness
That was to be her punishment.
Guilty of possession and distribution
Twenty-five years to life
How could they know she had never possessed
Anything worth the while
Had never distributed anything except pieces
    of herself

Which she gave freely
To those in need, or to those who, like
Her, were broken, and needed a fix?
She possessed nothing as they led
Her, handcuffed, away
What she left behind
Forlorn and weeping in the second row of benches
Were not her children,
Lost and desperate in the whirlwind

My head is filled with images
Of Melissa and me on the court steps
She crying and clinging to my skirt
Me crying and clinging to a distant God
As we made our way to the bus terminal
For the long journey home.
My head is filled with images
That mare at night and tear at my flesh
There is no rational corner in my head
Beyond making tea for Melissa
Beyond making conversation with Miss Ruby
Nothing to make my legs move in the
Direction of our apartment as if there

Were sense to moving

If anyone could look into my head

See or feel the dread that has captured

Me or see within this sad, unhappy brain

They would only turn away

Turn away.

MELISSA AMBERS

Mommy seemed a hundred miles away
In the yellow-light
Courtroom
With all of the people standing at the tables
And Mommy was smaller
Than they were
Even though everybody says
She is so tall
The judge pushed his glasses
Up on his nose when he was talking
But Mommy just looked
Down

When the judge said how
Long Mommy would be in jail
A terrible sound came out of
Junice

A hurt sound

A *Uhhh!* sound

Her body jerked forward

I was so scared

So scared

People were shuffling papers

They *swished* as people

Stood and their feet

Cluffed across the floor

Mommy turned

Her eyes were dark and

Wild as if she were

Seeing a monster coming

I turned to see what Mommy saw

But all I saw was the people leaving

Through the big doors in the back

When I turned back to Mommy

There was just a little piece of her left

Between the big policemen

My skin was crawling

And my arms were shaking

Miss Ruby called out in the courtroom

She said "Be strong, daughter!"
Junice said I was crying.
I don't remember crying but afterward
Afterward
My throat was sore

RUBY AMBERS

Yeah, it's hard, baby
It's hard right down to the bone
I said Oh, it's hard baby
It's hard right down to the very bone
It's hard when you're a woman
And you find yourself all alone
I've been flapping and scrapping
And running from door to door
You know I've been flapping and scrapping, honey
Running from door to door
I ain't what I used to be, ain't really Miss Ruby
   anymore
Oh, daughter, daughter, daughter,
Why you chasing White Girl dreams?
Yes, oh, daughter, daughter,
Why you chasing White Girl dreams?
Them rainbows you were finding,
Ain't really what they seems to be.

I told Junice to get herself on up
We ain't no trifling women
I been knocked down and flung around

"Junice, why you looking so sad, baby?
You got your Miss Ruby here, ain't you?
You and Lissa gonna be all right.
Miss Ruby's been scruffed and roughed
In her day but she don't lay down.
No sir. You mama will be home 'fore
You know it."

"She got twenty-five years, Miss Ruby."

"We Ambers women. We been down and we
Been up. We don't tip and run. No, we sure
Don't. I had your mama on a cold day
In December, thirty-some—how old is Leslie?
Never mind, you ask her when she come
Home."

"She got twenty-five years, Miss Ruby."

"When she come home we got to sit
Down and have a family talk. My
Aunt Louise used to say that once in
A while you had to have a family talk
Get into the Bible. You know Louise was
Always into the Old Testament. Your
Mama come home I'm going to tell her
About the Old Testament. Genesis, and
All that. We ain't had a family talk for
A while, but when she come home
We need to have us one. Get into the
Bible, and all that."

"She got twenty-five years, Miss Ruby."

JUNICE AMBERS *looking from the* WINDOW *of the* BUS

We drone along the faceless highway
That is the history of my life
Telephone poles, light poles, pretending
Differences, pretending they are not the
Thousand pages etched of who I am
Each episode was written by somebody
With my dark face, my broad back,
Mama, Miss Ruby, how far back do we go?
Did some Bantu gap-toothed woman
Rise one bright morning
And march willingly to the shore?
To the waiting ships?

We are on the Thruway
Miss Ruby, her mind slipping in and out

Of Knowing, chatters on while Melissa,
My sweet Melissa who already
Knows how to weep without
Tears, leans against the hard window
Passing neon lights play across
Her pretty face, her sadness
The trial is over, the sentence read
There are no comforts to share
No songs to ease our sorrow
Only the long bus ride home

LESLIE AMBERS *in*
BEDFORD HILLS PRISON

What are they doing to me? To me?
Groping and groping, reaching to see
If I have hidden my soul somewhere
Between my legs, not seeing it puddle
On the cracked grout floor
Of this steel tomb
They are calling this my forever home
"Hide your body along the green-gray
Walls," they say
"So we cannot see your crime-ugly face."
But I know they see everything
They want me not to see myself
But I must, I am desperate to see
My image, my wild eyes searching
For the high of being me again
Of being Leslie, of evoking
Ambers

On the streets of the city
They have taken my Who-I-Am
As well as my What-I-Was
And now I am desperate for them both
Again

"Hey, Princess 649178,
Time to Bend and Grin!"
"Why she think she a princess?"
"Hey, Princess, you got any children?"

"I have two daughters
The oldest is named Junice."

"Shut up! We don't care about your dumb family!"

"But you asked—"

"Yeah, but we don't care.
And neither do you, or you wouldn't be in here!"

Where is my daughter? Where is Junice?
Why doesn't she come flying through the walls

Screaming in rage and fury because of

What they are doing to me, to me.

Why doesn't she break this darkness into

A thousand crumbling fragments

And lift me over the razor wire cliffs

Of my despair?

Where is Miss Ruby, my mother,

With her roots and spells

Where are the black candles

That spell death to my enemies?

Perhaps they are on their way

Perhaps they are at the gates

"Shut up! We don't care about your dumb family!"

"But you asked—"

"Yeah, but we don't care.

And neither do you, or you wouldn't be in here!"

I care, I have always cared

Really.

JUNICE *tells her* STORY *at the* FAMILY WELFARE BUREAU

There was a time
When I thought of my life as a journey
Knowing somewhere there would be a place
At which I would Arrive and be
Beautiful
On clear days, if I shielded my eyes
Just right and squinted into the distance
I could almost see the station's sign
Bold and shining on a summer-green hill
But none of that was true

There were no tracks climbing
Like a silver arrow toward a place called
Future. No friendly tower or friendly faces
Eager for my appearance

No, it is all cycle and recycle
What the great-grandmother has done
Is to rut the earth for her children
What the grandmother has done
Is to widen the furrow for her children
What the mother has done
Is to square the pit
Deepening it for the ritual to come
And here I sit, grave deep among the
Waiting worms, staking my claim
As they stake theirs.

What do I want, you ask
What do I whisper to God
In the early mornings?
Only to keep Melissa safe
To hold her close
Away from the past, away from
The expectation in your eyes
Is this too much to ask?

DAMIEN *on a* BENCH
in the SCHOOL OFFICE

The bench in the office is four feet wide

So when she was there, elbows on her knees

There should have been enough room

Except for someone else's green backpack

Against the slatted side

Which barely left enough room

For me to sit, but I did

She looked up at me, and I smiled

She looked away

Fran leaning across the ledgers on the counter

Commented on my admission to Brown

"Your mother must be very proud."

I hear her sigh. Then she was called into

The inner sanctum

I could hear snatches of conversations

Words piled on her.

Must. Responsibility. Days missed from school.

She came out and sat down again
Elbows on knees.
Not noticing our hips touching
Or the current between us
"You want to stop for coffee?" I asked,
    surprising myself

JUNICE *on a* BENCH
in the SCHOOL OFFICE

I anchored myself on the bench
Waiting to be called into the office
The office clerks chirped Damien's name
Wonderful this, amazing that
The other side of the universe
He came in and sat next to me
Touching me, his legs stretched out
The Lord, waiting for his homage
Me in the office, hearing the words
Wond'ring if most of the world was like me
Listening to the judgments of others
The warnings, the I-Told-You-Sos
The sentences.
On the bench again, waiting for the written
Notification. He speaks.
"Coffee?" He says. "Why?" I ask. He shrugs, our
    hips are touching

I'm not your kind, I think.

"Some other time?" I say.

"Fine," He says. I search for words that seem
Softer. "The bench is small,"
I say. "That's all right," He says quickly,
His shy smile illuminating the answer.

"Can I call you?" He asks.

"Why?" I ask.

DAMIEN *and* KEVIN *and* JUNICE *in* *the* SUPERMARKET

Kev, there's Junice, I spoke to her yesterday
She strikes me as . . .

You hit on her?

No, man, we exchanged a few words, and . . .

And you laid out your line

I'm seeing her differently, you know

She's sweet, neat, and filet mignon
The best kind of meat

No, what I feel is that

Somehow she's more real than
I'm used to being around
It's as if I found something within me.

You're tripping, bro. She's a slick chick
I got to admit. She's as strong as she's
Long but I don't get the sudden vision
This heated rush that raises one dark
Flower, lovely as it is, above the
Bush.

Kevin, things are happening around me, man

Things that you expected

Right, and that I've never rejected

Things that happen according to a plan

And maybe that's what makes Junice shine
What makes her seem suddenly fantastic
Why in a garden that for all the world seemed mine
She is the only rose that doesn't smell of plastic

Look, there, see how she turns, how she touches
Her hair. How she gestures as if writing
Her name in the air.

Ah, new, strange, yes, I see.
A little slip and slide when
Roxanne is not around
A little grip and glide with
Someone new. I'm hip. If you had slipped
Me the 411 from the get-go
Then I wouldn't have thought you
Were losing it.

Kevin, you're never going to change
That girl is doing things in my chest
That make my heart happy and
I think that feeling in my stomach is my
Liver laughing to be alive again

If the feeling goes lower
You got my vote. But she's coming
This way. Now she sees us. She's smiling
She's yours, man. Rap her up and

Take her home if you want, but since
I got your back, let me stack some wisdom on
You. Give Junice some serious slack
Or give your mama a heart attack. And
That's a fact, Jack!

JUNICE *in* *the* SUPERMARKET

Melissa wants spaghetti
Miss Ruby wants chicken
But won't remember what she asked for
We have some beef left over and enough
On the card for onions, cheese, and rolls,
I'll make sandwiches
And not think of Damien
Who is he? High horsing into my life
And me teetering on the rim of the
Volcano, choking on its fumes

He strews his path with prose
And expects me to skip from verb to noun
Making garlands of his wit
How dare he hi-yo-Silver me when I am so
Needy, my palms turned up in begging
Lágrimas de luna por favor

The onions are perfect. Melissa
Will want to keep one on the kitchen
Table. A nine-year-old romantic
Wanting to be an Old Master

What can Damien want of me?
Once he smells the sulfur pouring
From my life he will run
When he reaches for my hands
And finds them wringing in hopelessness
He will shrink away. What does he know
Of my lips, twisted in cursing and defiance
What does he know of my body
Bent double with the weight of my days?
Won't he cringe and move away? Isn't that what
Men do to girls like me?
Cheese wrapped in plastic, colorless Wicca cheese
But good enough on leftover beef with
Fried onions and Goya sauce
Thinking he is a man, he invites me
To coffee. Thinking he is a moment away from the
Rage I have become, I will go
Hoping that I will not offer my heart

Too soon, or reach too greedily into
Promises neither of us can fulfill
Rolls, I must have rolls
The soft kind that Miss Ruby can manage
Damien appears sweet, as boys go, and offers
An untested heart. He needs a girl
Who thinks of love as June pleasant days
Or shopping
With nothing lost that cannot be replaced
But I am not that girl. I am Street
My needs are fierce. I am hungry
And my teeth are sharp. Where will he
Find the strength to hold me?
What can he bring to the vacant lot
Of my horizons
And whatever he brings
Will it be street enough to keep us safe
Against the storm?
Could it even withstand the voltage of
His mother's shock?

MELISSA'S DREAM

I was in the living room
Everyone thought my red dress
The one with the neat silk stitches
Was blue and Miss Ruby touched it
With her long fingers and sharp nails
And said I shouldn't wear locs because my hair
Wasn't strong enough to wear them
But I wasn't wearing locs, my hair was up
The way Junice had put it and so I put my
Head against her chest and
Listened to her heart
Ka-thump! Ka-thump! Ka-thump! And I wasn't
    as scared
Anymore and then some other people were
    walking
Around the room, only now the brown and purple
Rug was a wooden floor that sounded *shlud-shlud*
As people walked and everyone said not to mind

Because I looked so pretty in my blue-green dress
Only Junice knew I was wearing a red dress
Ka-thump! Ka-thump! Ka-thump! Again and again
  and again

The MOTHERS

ERNESTINE BATTLE

Damien is different, a tender
Boy with a heart too forgiving for its own dear sake
Uneasy with the higher way that for him
Is as natural as rain in spring
Not that he pretends to royalty or
Misunderstands his birth although that
Birth should not be denied, my side at least
Has made its mark in three eastern cities
And has been in *Who's Who* several times
Not that any of that matters because
It is my son's bright future that concerns
Me. I don't want it lost in the slanting
Chasm of this busy concrete forest
With its neon snares and jazzy traps
No, my son has a greater role to
Play than is offered on this
Meager stage.

LESLIE AMBERS

Junice favors me. Something about the mouth
The way she stands to her full height
The arch of her back. The length of those brown
Thighs that men capture in their minds long
Before they glimpse the reality of her womanhood
But she is naïve. Wearing her childhood around
Her neck like a laurel. At her age I had already lost
One child and she was on the way. Some would say
She's spoiled but I know she just hasn't
Found the fight in her as yet. We are scufflers
We in the Ambers clan.
We don't let each other down. She
Will fight by my side as I fought at Miss
Ruby's side. She knows what family means
And it's that meaning that concerns me.
No, there is more to her than
These walls, these cells, can stand against.

ERNESTINE

It is not the petty hustlers
Who worry me. He'll handle them

It's the unsuspected ones. Bright
And so clever in their come-ons
That he will think that he is the hunter
Not the hunted. Easy money
And easier pleasures waiting
For him to taste, to be enticed
By a pretty face, a quick and
Breathless conquest. He'll think it's love.
I know better

LESLIE

It's not the glaring mornings
That worry me. She'll handle them
It's the quiet nights alone, nights
In which she thinks that she is cold
Even as the radiator hiss
Fills the room or the August heat
Makes her sweat drip in the darkness
The nights will make her show herself
In moonlight as the hunter finds
Her in his sights. She'll think it's love.
I know there is no such thing.

ERNESTINE

I will not let him fall
In lust with some low child
With legs that run then fall
Apart as if surprised

Upon my solemn oath
As long as life is in
My bosom I will hold
Damien safe. I will!

LESLIE

Uh-uh, she won't fall
Not my Junice—or turn her back
On me when I am stuck
Inside these walls

Miss Ruby's mind is nearly gone
I got no one but my baby girl
Our destinies will go hand in hand
As long as there's breath in me

The FATHERS

AVERY BATTLE

When I was Damien's age I was hard
Not that the boy should be as rough as me
But I wish we could talk a little more
He could tell me of his dreams and what part
I might play in them, if I have a part
What with his mother hovering over
Him like a protective vulture. Too harsh—
She means him well, I know she means me well
But still, I sometimes wish he would find time
To talk a little more. That would be good.

ARTHUR WILLIAMS

I heard that Leslie got herself busted
For selling drugs—some heavyweight
Action somewhere upstate. Well, she was
Always sly and fly, chasing that big paper

Hey, that big paper brings some big time
You don't want the time—don't do the crime
That's the way the story goes
You got to check out where you strolling
You can't tell people how to live their lives.
Junice? Was that her girl's name?
How old is she? Ten? Eleven? She probably
Hanging with Leslie's mama.
Now that was a woman who could
Drink some gin. I tell you,
She could drink some gin.

JUNICE *and* MELISSA

I have to open my sister's mouth
And fill it with thoughts as hard
As stones so she can practice her lines
She needs to speak clearly
As she lies.
"Melissa," I will say
"Miss Ruby will run the house
She'll make fried chicken and okra
Hamburger and broccoli
And when her mental hat flies
Off down some weird and wondrous
Street she will not chase it
Will not ramble as she talks
Or twist fragments of the past
Into a hopeless stew of
Neverwasness. Miss Ruby will
Be our Strength and Center around which
We will build Family

Are you listening, Melissa?
Will you tell them how sure we are
Of our grandmother? Can you understand
That we sell the Shadow to support
The Substance of Miss Ruby?
And dear Melissa, you have to say it all with
Happiness in your voice. You must smile
Sweetly. It is always *Miss Ruby*
With a tilt of the head, and *Mama*
With love in your voice and—"

She left!

—Call her Mama!

She left, that's all to say

—One day we'll be with her again.

She left!

One day
If we hold on

Hold ourselves together
We'll find some way to bring her home
Again

Never
She walked away
To live in her own world
Junice, I hate her! She left us!
She did!

I know
Baby, I know
We have the same ragged
Steel tearing at our guts, ripping
Our lives
I know
Oh look
Into my eyes
There's fear, but there's fight, too
We can be more than we should be
We two
Just you and me
Melissa and Junice

Two strong Black women against all
That's wrong

Junice
I'm filled with scared
My stomach aches with sad
I believe in you, my Junice
I'll try

RACHEL DAVIS, DEPARTMENT *of* FAMILY SERVICES

I have a job to do, a thing, a chore
To look into, investigate, to know
What is happening, what's the score
What makes this family tick, what makes them go
And if there is a danger, then it must be seen
Put aside, taken care of, duly filed
With each detail revealed, all secrets seen
With the clear aim that what is intended
Is not some vague desire, no "if I could"
No debate, pointless and open-ended,
But that clear truth we call "the greater good."
There is no room for maybes when babies
Are involved and they are so young, these two
To be brought into family court
The younger girl crying, the older glares

But I only write the Final Report
I am not the *cause* of their despair
What they don't understand
Is that the precise list of regulations
Properly numbered and indented
Is family. They still long for blood and
Flesh although blood and flesh has failed
Them. The mother, Leslie, is my age.
The report says that she has a tattoo on
The side of her neck that says "Kitty."
I could never imagine myself with a
Tattoo, or selling drugs, or having
Children without a father at least listed
As Divorced.
At sentencing she pleaded that her
Children needed her, would be desperate
Without her. The judge asked her
Where were her children when she was
Out selling drugs? She had no answer.
Now she has given her family to the
State.
The girl is sixteen, and much like the mother
Her hair uncombed, her face looking older

Than it should, her eyes darting back and
Forth as she talks. She is a thinker,
But what does she think? Her mother
Is the kind who doesn't think, who pushes
Her way through a crowd of days
As if she were in a hurry to get somewhere
And yet turns at every obstacle to start in
A new direction.
My report will be straightforward, to the point.
Should the state intervene, wrap its arms
Around the girl and the sister? The sister
Is almost ten, and shy. I almost caught myself
Reaching out to her. Almost felt myself being
Stirred by her youth, the eyes that looked
Through me as if they could see
The cool marrow of my being.
Once she smiled for no clear
Reason and I felt that she had seen
The little girl in me that once was as
Pretty and hopeful as she is now.
And when she smiled I smiled back
But then . . . but then I knew I must
Move on and find that

Greater good.

The Final Report will depend on the
Grandmother. Can she care for these
Children? There is already a file on
Her, it is thick with yellowed papers
And the accumulation of forty years
Of dampness. Her Report, 1076-A,
Individual Court Record lists her
As Stokes, Ruby, aka Ambers, Ruby—
Black, two felony convictions.
Assaults, one with a knife, one with a
Bat against a man.

What kind of life
Is defined by felonies, by street
Fights? What can she give these
Girls? What can she contribute
To the greater good?

JUNICE *in* *the* EARLY MORNING

Miss Ruby has probably always been
Bigger than she needed to be
Square shouldered, skin dark and dry
As the black field dirt she came from
Wide hipped, wide lipped
Dried hard in the bitter Georgia sun
Somewhere along the hardscrabble road
Somewhere between the Left Alone
Blues and the One Room
Bathroom down the hall
The almost saved daughter
Of Sunrise Baptist Tabernacle
Hardened. One day the music
Was loud enough and the
Rhythm strong enough to
Push her too far into the Night

To ever turn back.
She is my flesh and blood,
Big boned as I am big boned
Uncomfortable in
Her skin.
Now she lives in shadow and memory
Her mind a cluttered shelf
In a narrow hallway closet
Her life is a tattered volume of fading
Photos, brown edged and crumbling
Some hopelessly stuck together
In her quiet times, between the pain
Of her newfound wilderness and the
Rage of not knowing who she is
She sorts the pictures, putting faces
With times, times with places
Sometimes, away from the girls who
People her life, she cries in the darkness
Thin shoulders, no longer straining
Against the twisted bra straps
Hunch forward. Dark hands twist
Her half-empty cup

Nervously as she waits for the silence
To stop its threats
For the talking to start the day.

"Morning, Miss Ruby."

"Go on, child."

"How you feeling today?"

"You know, there ain't no need complaining."

"You want some eggs?"

"They were all right."

"You didn't have any eggs yet, Miss Ruby. I'll make
   you some."

"You're so sweet, Kitty."

"Junice, Miss Ruby. I'm Junice."

DAMIEN *and* ROXANNE

"Roxanne, where you headed?" Damien asks.

"To the Computer Lab to see
If any He-males are sending
E-mails my way. Where are you going?"

"To the office to check out the yearbook
Pictures."

"Well, aren't you the busy one," Roxanne says,
"And by the way—Colson asked me to
The Charity Jam—something about
Homeless Asians, or Hurricanes—is there
A war in Angola? Or is that a prison?
Anyway, you've been so busy
Too busy for dances, I'm sure. Mother was
Surprised because she took it
For granted that you and I would be—

Well, you know how mothers are,
Taking things for granted and Cynthia
Said she saw you talking to that girl
Hummis, or Loomis, something like
That and don't they have such
Interesting names and did I hear her
Mother was a drug dealer—Oh, I guess that's
What you do when you get hot
Or is it ghe-tto. If you're not too busy
You should take her to
The Charity Jam. I'm sure she'd fit
Right in. Don't you think so?"

The PHONE CALL

Hello, Junice?
No, Damien Battle, Kevin's friend
We spoke just the other day, remember
In the principal's office. Yeah. Yeah.
Wondering if you were busy Friday
There's this dance at a club downtown, not hip
But good for a laugh, something new to do
Could you? Could we? I don't know. Are you free?
It could be fun. Something to do. You and me.

Damien, it's good to hear from you
Friday, no, I can't.
I have to babysit. You called so late
Perhaps some other time. It sounds all right.
But I thought you and Roxanne were tight
She seems more your type. Nothing personal.
And I'm glad you called and everything
But right now I'm a bit unglued

I love to dance, but not right now
I'm not really in the mood

Roxanne and I are friends, there's nothing more
Our folks go back, you know how that thing goes
But, hey, you want to stop at the coffee shop
I'm thinking of taking over the world, and I can
Use some advice.
Why am I holding my breath?
She's said "yes," why am I nervous?

DAMIEN, JUNICE,
and MELISSA
in GRACE'S COFFEE SHOP

How are things with you, He asked

You don't know? She responded

I've heard, He said

What? She asked.

That you are bruised, that there are tender spots in

Your life

There are no tender spots, She said, No bruises,

    She protested

(She put two teaspoons of sugar

Into her coffee, slowly stirring

Only the top)

The coffee used to be 50 cents here

Now it is a dollar, He said.

It's cleaner now, She said

The coffee is better

There used to be flies, She said
The flies liked the old coffee
He said
Her face flashed with smiling
(She looked away and then back at him
Delighted with his joke
He wanted to delight her again.)
Things change, She said
Her face darkening with her mood
Bruises happen.
Sometimes, He said, it's hard to know
How to handle things

(Melissa was quiet, but she was thinking
That sometimes words
Danced instead of talked
They bowed and touched
And moved away
Making spaces in the air
Between them
It was hard to know what
Damien and Junice were talking about
Unless you could read the shape

Of the air between
Them. Melissa looked, and guessed
That they liked each other.)

When will I see you again? He asked, reaching for
The bill.

When would you like? She replied
Looking toward the far counter

Friday? He asked.
Okay, She said, with a shrug of one
Shoulder.
I'll give you my address, she said.
You can come by. I'm
Babysitting you-know-who.

Fine, He said.

(Melissa smiled)

But my crib is just a crib, Junice said
No *Home & Garden* stuff, just "do get by"

But if you still want to come,
Then ring the bell

(What am I doing? He'll take one quick look
And wish he was anywhere else but here
I'm already ashamed of what I think
He will think of me, of the life I lead)

I'll see you Friday

DAMIEN *standing on* the **PLATFORM,** *waiting* *for the* **UPTOWN 2**

What sweet surprise have I found in her
That makes me high with gladness?
That makes me want to babble to my lost saints
And count the ways to celebrate her wonder?

I see Melissa softly touch her arm
And I long to speak the language of that touch
The hum and thrum of crosstown traffic sings to her
And I long to scat and jazz that ode of joy

Her smile lifts and lightens me, and I want to fly
My newfound wings slanting to a sky
Ablaze with shimmering brilliance
As I am ablaze and silly and rapt

Why does her look startle me?
I have seen eyes sparkling in a sideways glance
Why do her lips, pouting in a gentle curve
Make my brain reel and my heart dance?

With Junice I am not merely Damien
But something new, a me invented
Each atom of my being alive with feelings
And oh what sweet sensations

The crowded station rattles and shakes
But I am alone on the mountaintop
Naming the creatures of the earth
And this sweet creature, this Junice, I will call Love

JUNICE *washing* DISHES

He might not show at all, but if he does
I will take his jacket, and ask him to sit
Where will he sit? On the sofa, of course
He'll look right at me, too polite to stare
At the peeling walls or the faded rug
He'll ask how I've been and I'll say "Quite well,
Thank you." Then I will have to sit, but where?
Next to him on the sofa seems too bold
But the window seat is too far away
As if I'm afraid to be close to him
Or being too respectful. That's not good, either.

Miss Ruby hardly touched her food
And she doesn't eat at all if I
Put out the good plates. It's as
If her mind is back to some party
From a hundred years ago.

If Damien brings food I'll have to sit near him
Melissa will be watching television
And Miss Ruby will be asleep.
I hope she doesn't snore

I'll make small talk, something about school
Look at me, telling myself I don't care
What he thinks yet planning every move
He'll sit there and I'll sit here with nothing
Between us except our good intentions.
And he had best bring his good intentions
If this boy thinks I'm easy, some chump chick—
I'll start my good-byes at the end of hello
Maybe I'll just meet him at the door
And tell him I've changed my mind
And asking him here was just
A mistake, a stumble of the mind
Like when the wrong word comes
From the lips, or a face looks
For a moment familiar but then,
Up close it's clearly strange.
In a way I resent him,
Sweeping across the desert of my life

With his cooling waters

Letting the blazing whiteness of his

Sails fill the horizon as my arms grow

Weary of the tide. Damien looks at

Me as if he is thirsty

And I want to be a river

He looks at me as if he is hungry

And I want to leap upon his tongue.

He makes me want to write

His name across the lines

On my yellow pad. I write

"Damien loves . . ." and leave

A space for another name.

JUNICE *and* MELISSA

Hey girl
You were in bed
And we did have a talk
Or don't you remember little
Sweetheart?

I know
We talked and all
But can't I take a peek
He ain't made of gold or nothing
Is he?

No, but
He is special
He does the kind of things
That I wish that he were doing
With me

Junice

That boy has got

All up inside your head

You're going to be in luv tonight

Big-time

Away!

Back to your bed

You're talking like a child

It's Junice I have to handle

Not him

DAMIEN

Junice moves uneasily through the room
Her stops punctuated by a soft smile
That sends shivers of delight up my spine
My smile doesn't fit my face anymore
Clumsily I try to hold the space
She gives me between the yellowed curtains
And the darkly stained table where my legs
Cross and uncross searching out casual
The smell of food cooking in some other
Kitchen reminds me that we share the world

Junice moves uneasily through the room
I speak, and her quick mind catches the thought
And tosses it playfully at my feet
I am eager to laugh and she knows it
I talk nonsense and she nods, I babble
And she babbles back. I am excited
Yes, and afraid to be in her presence

In the faraway next room there are sounds
"Melissa's watching some kiddie program,"
Junice says. "I bribed her to waste her mind."

We are dancers, she with bare feet
And dangling bracelets, the native child
Burned by the copper sun
I am the explorer
Discovering that there are two
Sides to the ocean

"Damien, what are you thinking?" she asked.

"I am thinking that I am not thinking.
What are you thinking?"

"I am thinking that I am thinking too much,"
    she said.

"Is that good or bad?" I asked.

"I don't know," she said, freezing the thought
I stood and put my arms around her

She put her head against my chest
In the long moment that followed
It was impossible to breathe
Too difficult to speak
We were rapt in each other
For a handful of heartbeats
Until, embarrassed, she pushed me away
We had shared more
Than we knew possible
Then I was standing, jacket in hand, at the door
Awkwardly we faced and wondered if Could
Would turn to Yes, her fingertips kissed
My face. My lips barely parted and quickly
Closed.
Down the stairs, and into the cool night
A half-moon floated
High above the jutting chimneys
Perhaps there were two moons
Perhaps a dozen

JUNICE *at* BEDFORD HILLS *to* *see her* MOTHER

What will I say to her? Hello, Mother?
Where will I put my eyes when they don't smile?
Will I say that Melissa cries for her
In the darkness? That she calls her name
As the night creeps into the cold gray day?
What will I say to her? Hello, Mother?

The package I left at the desk—panties
The bra she wanted, tampons in a box
A card from Miss Ruby—is not enough
To bridge the distance between
Us. If sorrow were a shawl
We could share it against the cold

What will I say to her? Hello, Mother?

Will I be able to touch her, to kiss
Her cheek and tell her amusing stories?
The guards search me, tossing my confidence
Into the brown plastic bag with my keys
Reminding me that I am Black
That I am lesser.

Shuffling
Through the gates with the others
Flinching
As the doors slam behind me
I think of Damien, glad he's not here
Letting my thoughts anchor to him
What would he think?
Wide-eyed, his mind bouncing
Madly from green-gray wall
To green-gray wall

"Hello, Mama," I force the words out.
"How are you?"
She tries to smile, but can't
Her mouth opens and I know she has
Practiced what to say but she can't control

The torrent of words that gush forth

I'm fine, and you? Have you spoken to a lawyer?
What are you doing out there? What are you doing?
Don't you care about me? I'm your mother!
Did you bring any money? Commissary
Costs money. Don't you know that? Don't
    you know?
I can't stand this place. Get me out of here!

She is a wolf caught in a trap,
Gnawing at the foot that holds her
She growls at me and yelps in pain
Her eyes bleed tears
And yes, she is my mother
And YES, she is my mother!

You can't turn your back on me. Don't you know
I spent nine months with you and . . .
I need a good lawyer for my appeal
Don't you know this place is crazy, listen
To what they're saying. Talking about home
As if they are ever going. What are . . . ?

Head down, I admit to doing nothing.
The blizzard of her hurts falls heavily
And I am beaten. Sensing the welling tears
She stops to breathe. Her tone softens

Are you doing well in school? Having fun?
Does Melissa do her homework at night?

"There is a boy," I say. "His name is Damien
Just the thought of him cheers me
Gives me power over the uncaring
Hardness of the hood, over the secret thoughts
That insist on having their way with me."
Her eyes go wild
Her fingers clench
Her voice becomes a muted shriek

How can you do this? How can you leave me?
Oh, my God, you are a terrible thing!
You're grinning with some fool while your mother
Your mother rots in this Godforsaken
Place forever and you don't care forever and I
Hate him forever and I hate you what are you

Doing? They're taking my life!
I want my life back. They didn't tell me
They could take it. They could just take it!

The screaming goes on
Like nails scratching across my heart
A heavy woman complains that she
Cannot hear her brother
And she needs the news because she's going
To be in the World soon and then a guard
Round faced, bored, lumbers over and hits
His baton on the table between us

The hour has ended and I am drained
"There are bruises in your life," Damien said
I long for him.
On the bus headed southward
My tears somehow signal a tattooed man
To sit with me. When his hand finds my leg
I know I have found my passage to Hell
Wearily I push the hand away
And try to sleep

JUNICE *and* MELISSA *at* HOME

Melissa peers
Deeply into my eyes
Looking for clues that everything's
All right

All right
She spoke of you
Something about homework
I told her you were doing well
She smiled

She smiled
Then read your note
And put it to her chest
Then she read it aloud again
I lie

KEVIN *and* DAMIEN
in KEVIN'S HOUSE

Yo, Damien, are you okay? Your eyes
Have a distant glaze and you've been
Walking in a daze for days. Tell me
What's up? What's going down?
Is something going around that I
Need to know about?

Kevin, my main rooter
Mighty square shooter
My head is spinning
For no apparent reason

Hey, man, it's flu season
Asian, Avian, Three Day, too
You need some serious chill out
Get the heating pad and pills out
Some hot tea and TLC

Should make the sadness flee.
And if all that
Don't juice your feelin'
You better cop some penicillin!

No, little brother,
There's no bacteria
In the area, it's Love
That lifts and gifts
This mortal

Damien, excuse me if you will
Abuse me if you must
But take me into your trust
And tell me that this plan
Does include the fair Roxanne?

Roxanne, do I know her?

Do you *know* her?
If you don't know the child
Your mother has chosen
Tell me just what has frozen

Your logic?
Maybe I'm completely wrong
Your new love is vehicular
Or something strictly testicular
Or you've downloaded some song
That has turned your brain
To mush

Junice, Kevin, Junice
I have found her
And she has found me

Old friend, cut buddy, my splib on the rib,
Have you taken Junice to your mama's crib?
And do you have exact words
Passed down from above
Just how do you know that you're in love?

Yesterday a woman smiled at me
No, she smiled at my own mad smiling
As I walked and spoke to myself
Spoke and answered as if I were surprised
At what I was saying, at what I was feeling

And what I was feeling was the wonder
Of being more than me, of being more
Than mere here and now allowed
I had become a shining star, a burning nova
Exploded with love
Flying through an endlessly
Expanding universe
Away from the me that was
Toward a me that is beyond
Understanding.

Yo, you're right, my man
I don't understand it either
But it's definitely heavy

JUNICE *thinks of* *calling* DAMIEN

Hello, Damien, yes this is Junice
I'm calling because this many-cornered
Room is pressing in on me so hard
That I feel I will be crushed. Yes, something
Happened today. I received a notice
From the Department of Health Services
Saying that for the greater good of all
Concerned they would have to assume complete—
Damien, I can't say the words. Even
Though I have practiced them, have let their taste
Fill my mouth with their acid apathy

What can you do? I don't know. Can you fly?
Change yourself into the wonder of all
Things? Blaze truth to the world? Can you become
A wild beast that chases demons away?
A flowing stream that carries poor meek girls

To comfort? Are these things that you can do?
Have I been crying? No, but I have screamed
Sorrow to the wind and rained misery
To the pavement beneath my window
I don't know if that's the same as crying
Damien, I am searching for myself
In the flickering shadows of despair
I have become invisible, there's just
The sound of my voice echoing against
The empty streets where once I pretended
To be. I am loose in space, and falling.

And the Waiters wait for me, mouths open
Remembering the taste of the others
Miss Ruby, Leslie, mothers and daughters
I see myself on the report, sixteen-
Year-old girl without parental guidance
Or resources. I am on the menu.
What will I do? Grab the thin summer air
And hold it before my chest like a shield
Run down the busy streets, shouting havoc?
Fly with Melissa to the river's edge
And dare the tide to carry us away?

I am like a rat, scurrying across

The rooftops, my mind scritching and scratching

In its panic, my limbs digging fiercely

Into the red brick of the tenements

I am Street and I do not go easy

I am Street and I will not flinch from pain

I am Street! My mind and my soul are Street.

But my heart, this poor timid thing that beats

Behind these small breasts, betrays its owner

Telling her fingers to call Damien

Damien, are you there? Can you become?

Damien, are you there? Can you become

The hope I need? Can you help me be

More than it is written in my future

Or past? Is there another me to find?

JUNICE *calls* DAMIEN

Hello? How are you?
I saw my mother today.
She's all right, I guess.
She's down. It's to be
Expected.
Me? I'm all right.
You were thinking of me?
No, I'm not down. It's
Just a cold. Yes, and a
Headache. I'll wrap myself
Warmly, and think of you.
Good night, darling.

DAMIEN *in his* ROOM, *his* MATH HOMEWORK *on his* DESK

The phone is quiet in my hand
I imagine her brown cheek against
The white pillow. Her voice still echoes
In my head. I have never heard a voice
Like hers before, had never heard
The sound of a life scraped
Raw and left to shake and bleed
In the wind.
And if I have never heard that sound
That cry filtering through the storm
Where have I been? What music drowns
The cry? And yet . . . and yet . . .
As I sit in my room,
Wondering how to be heroic
Rummaging through my life

For a proper script
I am afraid. Afraid for all the
Things I should have said
Of all the words I sensed and
Refused to hear as her voice
Reached out to me.
In the ticktock
Quiet of my room, there is the
Low burrrrr of a crumbling shield.
Junice talks of Street.
Is Street the same as Hero?
Is Hero the same as Man? Is Man
The same as Damien?

JUNICE *at the* FAMILY COURT OFFICES

"No, I don't mean to be hostile

Ma'am.

It's just that I'm afraid that no matter

How loudly I speak

You won't be able to hear me

You say I can have no hand in

The decision. But look at these hands

They have scrubbed mats on the banks of
    the Congo

They lifted Moses from the bulrushes

These hands can crush razor blades

And catch sunbeams

They part rocks and turn back rivers

Does that make sense to you?

You say that your hands are tied

Can I beg them free?

You quote paragraphs and sentences
And laws with numbers and subsections
Will my tears erase them?
You say my family has a History
And wash your hands
As I am crucified to it
You are a woman, and I am a woman
Yes, it is relevant
You are Black and I am Black
Yes, it is relevant!
I'm sorry, I didn't mean to scream
I know it won't help my case
Miss Davis, ma'am, all I'm asking
Is for the chance to be stronger
Than the women in my family have been

My grandmother, once fierce,
Nods in her own world while
She waits for the next one
Did you see Leslie's eyes? Wild beyond tears,
Beyond pain, past hurting
I will tear that History apart.
All I need . . .

MISS DAVIS

I'm sorry, but I know you'll do well.

We'll make every effort to keep you and your

Sister together. Sometimes things can be

Arranged but there are no promises.

The Letter of Determination

Will be handed down in twelve days

And then we will know

We will have the answers in hand

And then we can move on from there

It's not up to me, you see

My hands are tied.

But may I give you some advice?

I see you have brought a young man

With you. Remember that your mother has no

Husband, just babies

Yes, and a History

JUNICE

Damien, I am lost
Did you hear her, how could she keep talking
    through
That fixed smile, that frozen face
The narrow head that kept turning away from me
Why doesn't she give me a chance?
Look, now we are walking down the same street
We took coming here. Time has passed, people have
Been born and some have died
But everything is the same. The sunlight haze .
Sweeps across the concrete
Framing the rhythms of souls lost in their
Own lives, but for me nothing
Has changed.

She has given you a date. Something about
    twelve days

An execution date. Everything will be over then

Will be determined.

When my mother came out of her

Mother's womb, Black and skinny, and screeching

When the doctor who delivered her skipped

The box naming a father

When the gypsy cab came and picked them

Up to make the drive to Alphabet City

When the smell of reefer rose sweet

And pungent through the gray project walls

When my grandmother called her friend to come

To see the new baby and no one was home

Everything was already determined

The steps are there, we just have to follow

Them to whatever doom there is

I have to think, he said

There is nothing to think about, Damien

What logic stands against logic?

I want to raise my sister and break the

Chains that bind us even though I know

Those chains cannot be broken

What logic sets that right except the rightness

Of denial? How will I discover how to

Defy gravity? How to fly over truths?
I have no money and without money there
Will be no way of living. What can you
Think of that will deny this? Do you think for
One moment that I want what is best for
Me? For Melissa? Reason spits in my face
With its sassy presence. I don't have a
Better reason than the book Miss Davis held
Before her small bosom like a hand-me-down Bible.
I am too real not to know that real will kill me
I am too street not to know what the streets hold
    for me

Let me think
Thinking is all I have
If wisdom is a pretense
Then let me pretend to be wise

Go. Think. Turn black into white.
Night into day. I am tired of thinking.
I know where it will lead me and I don't
Want to be there.
Go love. Do your thinking.

DAMIEN *by* HIMSELF
on the CORNER

Junice turns and walks away
Through the familiar shifting rhythm
Of a Harlem crowd

I have never felt so alone
Cogito ergo sum; I think, therefore I am
Dead thoughts in a dead language
What good is thinking? What good is *I am*
If *I am* is not something larger
Than I could ever be alone?
The thinking, the furrowed brow
Had always been, until this time
A comfort.
To this very moment every
Red horizon produced a new day
Every cloud its cleansing shower
The sun never stopped its

Brilliant arcing across my blue skies
What strange land have I entered
Where tsunami questions roar and crush the soul
And the gravity of the blood moon pulls no
Answers from the brooding tide?
What is there to think about
To weigh carefully
That Junice and Melissa enter
Some benign level of Hell
And what if Hell is not so Hellish
As it won't be once I put it
Beyond my sight, into the cool
Regions of intellect. If Hell
Is not so Hellish once out of
My mind, what will life be,
When I am out of Junice?
Comfortable? Without a doubt.
Carefully planned? To the last letter.
Life will resume, the too-familiar
Curtain rises once again, but
I've forgotten all my lines.
More important than what happens
To me, for the first time

In my life more important than
What happens to me, is what will happen
To Junice?
Can I shut my eyes, seal my ears
Not know what she stutters through
Her tears
That every distance
From love is too far? That every
Battering of the heart is impossible
To heal, and that a lifetime
Of shielding the wounds
Is too high a price to pay?
Junice has laid down her dreams
For the world to see
While I still clutch mine to my bosom
And whine my prayers to a God
Who wants more
Of me than I can bring to Heaven's door.

SLEDGE *and* DAMIEN *and* HARLEM *in front of* JACKIE ROBINSON PARK

SLEDGE

Yo, ballplayer, where you been hiding?

They put up two neon signs downtown and

Neither one of them spells out your name

You skipping the race or setting the pace

On up to the Big Time and putting

Down the little folks?

What, you ain't speaking?

I saw you with Junice, bro.

You liking that tall mama?

DAMIEN

Liking? You're not deep enough to understand

Anything deeper, so I'll say I'm liking her

SLEDGE

Yo, if you're talking about love
You must be slipping or tripping
Skirts are made for lifting
Not gifting with no emotion
Or are you Doing the Right Thing
Getting on the Bus and all that
Zing-zing kind of fling White dudes
Be talking about?

DAMIEN

Hey, I'm in love, Sledge,
But I don't expect you to dig it
They don't keep love in the sewers
You hang in

SLEDGE

Yo, Damien, I know her situation
She's just part of the booty nation
She'll be out here tricking
When the rent is due. Or don't you get the clue

When you see that her mama
Resides with the Upstate Brides?

DAMIEN

Sledge, you are just another turd
Who hasn't heard the word that the
Flushing is done. Take your stink
Someplace else, man. I don't have
The time for your mental grime.
What could you know about love?

SLEDGE

Yeah, you in love. And with your higher
Brain you got her higher parts
While I had to settle for those holding
Me close and whispering my name
Over and over.

DAMIEN

Watch your mouth, fool!

SLEDGE

If you feel froggy, come jump in my direction
If you feel like a soldier, march on over
If you needy, come get some of what I'm
Handing out by the fistful

Then there are two stallions
Standing toe to toe
One's breath warming the face of the other
Sliding past the emotional pains they
Can't express to the physical pains they
Can.
Then they fight. Fists fly, legs spread
Damien's fury forcing Sledge to back up
As he wards off the blows. Sledge goes
For the groin. The two roll on the
Cracked cement as children watch, never
Putting down their sodas, their bags of chips
It is just the everyday violence of a
Ghetto afternoon. Suicide bombers expressing
I-amness.
Damien pounds away. Basketball muscles
Are quick, his hands are even quicker, but

Sledge goes into his sock and pulls his shank.
Its arc is quick and the spurt of
Blood is a thin red bird in the slanted
Light of late afternoon
Suddenly the two warriors are apart, standing
Sledge, his breath coming in deep gasps,
His eyes bloodshot and wide, stumbles away from
The kneeling Damien.
"He's cut!" a child calls out.
"It ain't deep," is the knowing reply.
Damien feels the wound that has made a thin
Line along his jaw. The child observer was right
It wasn't deep. A trickle of blood
Runs down the neck and into the collar
Of his open shirt.

"Excuse me, young man, I see you are on
Your knees," a homeless man interrupts. "If
You're finished praying perhaps you could
Give an old man a dollar or two for a sandwich."

Damien's glance is angry. The homeless man
Amused. The children move to the jungle gym

Only Damien feels abused.

Damien stands for a while on the corner. Across the

Street two policeman sit in a squad

Car and look in his direction. If he had been

Hurt seriously they would have come over

Would have done whatever necessary for the

Greater good of the community. He starts down the

Hill, not planning to go but going

Not knowing what he wants to know

But knowing, looking and not looking

Until he reaches her block.

When she appears, head down

Groceries hugged against her chest

He calls her name and she stops, half in her

Doorway, her keys still pointed away from

The street, almost spilling the onions.

JUNICE *and* DAMIEN

What happened? She asked. You're a mess.

Do you know Sledge? He asked.

He exists, She said. But you've been hurt, come
    upstairs
I'll wash your face. What happened?

I just fought Sledge, and lost, He said.

Why?

He said he had made love to you.
I needed to shut his lying mouth.
To put the lie to his lay.
I knew you would never go with him.
He pulled a knife. But that doesn't matter now.

What matters now?

All I need is to hear the words from your lips to
    move on,
To stumble past his profanity.
Just tell me you are who I know you are.

What are you saying?
What words do you want from my lips? Words
That say that Sledge has not touched me? That I
Am pure? Unused? Excused? Unabused?
    Unconfused?
Is that how you are defining me? What is it that
    you want?
Some girl of your dreams with fairy-tale themes
Spouting from her lips? I am not the virgin version
    of your
Life, Damien. I am only what you see, this stick
Of a woman trying to make enough magic
To negotiate the shadows of these streets. You want
To name me according to my abuser, when I am only
Me. I can't use it. My life is not packaged,

Not tidy. There are leftover strands and jagged
Edges that cut even my friends. Blame Sledge if
    you must
Or God if you still trust in Heaven
Damien, I believed in you because I
Want to believe in the love I feel for
You. If that's not enough
I'm sorry. I'm sorry.

Damien walks away,
There is a stinging pain in his face
There is even more hurt within
The tall body, suddenly
Doubt-weakened, unsure, pushing
One foot before the other, an alien
Pushing through the underbrush
Of his own planet.
At home he finds his room
The four corners of his bed, his quilt
And under the quilt, his darkness
But in the landscape of his once-friendly
Mind there are only strangers

Coming at him with visions
That distort his world

Here are the Sledges hate-hating their way
Through life, mocking tenderness with their
Leering grins.
Here are the Regulators, who check their
Passions at the time clock, *tsk-tsk*ing their
Way to Pensionville.
Here is the Artist, snip-snipping from
His own memory (call it history)
Making his own portrait of her.

The night carried a thousand dreams
One moment the violence of his fight
With Sledge had him ripping at the covers
The next found him still and trembling inside
The coolness of the sheets, listening to the
Echoes of Junice's words as she walked
Away from him . . . away from him.

DAMIEN *and* *his* MOTHER *on* SATURDAY MORNING

Damien, I spoke to Kevin's mother
(Toast and tea on a tray)
He told her/she told me
You're in love with a girl
Is she a nice girl? Kevin's mother said/he said
Jail/drugs/mother/said/sister, too

I know you won't like her, I thought

Who knows what is right/wrong/good/bad
These days? Did you want eggs?

She is on the verge of bubbling over
Restless in the invisible cage she paces

As if it were a frame and she the vision
It encases. The voice rises in pitch.

We all must choose/pay dues/even though
Choice is not always easy/queasy/feelings
But nevertheless/I confess/the biggest mess is
    when we
Let our emotions/notions/devotions to causes
Change us/rearrange our lives in strange ways

Her hands move nervously, spilling
The tea onto the paper napkin

You have a station in life, education, the dedication
Of your father and me, you do know how much
We care, we have dared to care all these years
You can't just turn/spurn/burn your bridges
I missed your basketball practices?
Have you started your season yet?

Her name is Junice, I said.
She is Black, but comely

She brings me to places I haven't been
Before, other sides of far horizons

She is an unfortunate girl

She swallows rainbows
And when I put my head against her
Breasts, I hear music

Infatuation is a situation that maturation
Shows us must fail in the long run/bright sun
Of hard truth, Damien
You owe us the fruits of our sacrifices
Our turning away from worldly vices
To give you all the advantages and advice
That would carry you beyond beyond
It would be a terrible thing for you to
Surrender your life for some girl that I
Hate and I do hate her if she is going to
Ruin your life and after all you are my
Son and that has meaning. You have a life
And you just can't leave it. You just

Can't leave it lying in some gutter or some
Cheap hotel room with some girl who is no
Mystery, Damien, she is no mystery! The way those
People live. It's just the opposite of how we
Live. Her mother's life is just evil! Is that
What you want? Look at her history!

The screaming goes on
Goes on,
I shut out her voice, her words
But can't escape
Their awful weight

He spoke to himself
Listened to his heart
Mumbled through the tears

Yes, she is the fruit that will
Sustain me and yes, she brings
A rain that I know can chill
But it is a rain so sweet and sings
A song my soul insists

That I follow, if I would exist
As more than I have ever, ever been
If my mother calls it evil, then I embrace the sin

Damien turned away to find a place within
Himself to hide, knowing that hiding was no
Answer. His mother, a woman betrayed,
Locked in the prison of her frustration,
Continued through the night
His father joined the chorus
As they sang songs of
Well-Meaning/Parental/Hallelujahs
All-Encompassing Wisdom
With an occasional blues riff
To show that they were
With It
Sleep, hard coming, dream-filled
Gnawed at the night
The too-hot autumn smothered him
With self-doubt as what he knew
Tortured all he felt

DAMIEN *wakes at* NIGHT

It came to him
Like a cold rush of a wave
On a dark and foggy beach
Shocking the senses
Dazzling the brain

And when he had caught his breath
Had regained his balance
Had clawed his way through sleep to
Wakefulness
He saw clearly and finally
That nothing he had thought about her
Mattered
Not that she was soft
Or firm, or sweet or wondrous beyond compare
Not that her smile
Sang to his heart
Or that her voice

Soft against the hard jazz of the city
Filled him with a delight he had
Not thought possible, no
It was the becoming that he loved
The becoming of him and her,
Of Junice and Damien, and what more they
Could be together than he had ever dreamed
Alone.
It was not just the girl
He loved, but the Them
Of them, the city shape of them
The hard concrete of them
Against the dark-blue sky of them
The sweet promise of them
Of them, and them
And them
Them

NINE *a.m.* DAMIEN
calls JUNICE

The phone ringing, Damien sits cross-legged
On his bed, wondering what to say
The phone ringing
Forever in your arms
Is where I want to be
Holding you close
Within the space
That once held only me
The phone ringing
Forever in your warmth
The place for me and you
I feel the sun
Our life's just begun
I know you feel it too
The phone ringing
No one answering

DAMIEN *at* JUNICE'S DOOR

He listened for her footsteps, heard a distant radio,
A creaking sound, Miss Ruby filling the doorway
"Junice ain't here," she said. "Maybe she's at
    church."
He imagined drawing a line along the tops of
Miss Ruby's shoulders, another through the hips,
And wondered in what dimension they would meet
"You know it's Sunday," she said.
"And she ain't really gone, just out for the
    moment.
Just away. Maybe church, or maybe just away
From heartbreak. You know how you people
Like to bring heartbreak to a woman's door,"
Miss Ruby said. "And what was your name
    again?"
Damien wrapped himself in despair against
The cold wind, merciless as it lifted off the

River and pushed its way crosstown.
There was so much to say to Junice, he knew
And so little time to fit the words into his
Mouth.
His stomach churned, ached
For Junice, for her to hear his
Please, his pleas, his desperate "I love you"
The passion in "I need you so much!"
He went home and called her from his
Room
He called her as he walked down the
Street, searching passing faces
Looking for her eyes, all the
While trembling inside, trembling
That it might already be too
Late. She might have taken
Her heart to another place.

KEVIN *and* DAMIEN *on* MALCOLM X BOULEVARD

Damien, where have you been, bro?
I've been seeking and peeking
Around the corners and down
The streets since I heard that you and
Sledge had a serious throwdown
What was that about, man?

Issues, my pride in myths
Against his emptiness
I put love and Junice in the
Same breath and Sledge,
Whose soul barely peeks above
Indifference, scoffed and clawed
At the idea of it.
In the end, with no chance of
Winning, we both slunk away with
Our tails and tales between our legs

With only the children watching
Applauding our violent dance

Junice said something about a wound
But I see you're merely scratched

You saw her? You spoke to her?
I've been calling, but there's been no answer

I thought you knew
She's going to Memphis

Tennessee? When?

Tonight. What will you do?

Go after her.
What airline is she going on?

She's walking the dog, man
Greyhound. Tonight at nine.
But hear me. Hear me though
The words are coming up like

Blood from my throat because
I don't want to speak them.
You can't chase her, Damien.
You'd have to surrender your life
She doesn't know what she's going to
Do. All she got down there is an old woman
With an older Bible who might take them
In. Give them a room, a roof
The squareness of walls. But her
Situation sounds impossible.

It's impossible for her to stay here
To surrender Melissa to a system
That doesn't love her. To put
Her own oar into the waters of that
System.

What will you do if you find her?

Stay with her forever. Longer
If God chooses.

Damien. I love you like a brother, but
You can't do this.

There is an excitement about Junice
I feel it when I see her, I sense it
In your voice. But excitement is not
Enough, it is not a Forever cast

True, my brother, but the flash of
Danger that surrounds this girl
Illuminates her spirit
Like lightning zagging across
The rooftops on a steamy August
Night
And in that terrible flash
I see a spirit too noble to
Put aside. And the angel of her
Presence, too precious not to love
Standing in the only
Path left for me to take

Damien, what will you do?

Gather my courage, scrape together my
Resolve, withdraw all the character I can
Muster, and go after her. Maybe in Memphis
I can find the hope of an answer, or the

Certain pain of failure. Otherwise
It's all nothing but the constant stumble
To the grave. Wish me luck, bro.

Damien, I got your back
Wherever you are I'm going to be
There with you. I'm not a praying dude
But I'll be talking to the Man for you
Two. You deal with the Memphis
End, and count on me to be
Here. To the end, Damien.

And on from there, Kevin.
And on from there.

The **PORT AUTHORITY BUS TERMINAL**

The New York bus terminal is dark
Is dark despite the garish lights assembled
Along the tiled walls. Dark as if,
As if some malignant spirit has settled
Down with the tortured souls that rest
There until the police move them.
As if the desperate late-night travelers
To Salt Lake City and Savannah
And Memphis don't deserve the brightness
Of hope.
On the lowest floor, among the shuffling
Ragged and hairy men, families guarding
Cardboard boxes and plastic shopping
Bags, Damien found Junice.
Sitting next to an old man
Brazil-nut brown on the hard bench
His legs as restless, as aimless

As his restless, aimless tongue
She caught her breath when she
Saw him, turned quickly
Away.
Melissa peered wide-eyed around her
Sister's shoulder.
"Memphis is a special place," the old
Man said, remembering a distant brawl
Of nights and thinking it might have
Been Memphis. "Good people fall in
That town, but only strong people rise again."
Damien sat next to Junice
Knowing she could feel his warmth through
The space between them.

DAMIEN *and* JUNICE

Junice

Damien I don't want to see you.
I'm so glad you came.
I don't want you to say good-bye. Good-bye
I need to be brave, now. I'm so scared

I'm going with you

You're not strong enough. Go back
Home. I love you, but go back home.
You belong in a safer place. There's
So little for me in Memphis, a distant relative,
A life I don't know. You need to be safe.
It's all I want for you. Don't kiss my fingers.

Junice, there's no leaving in me.
No gentle grieving and going on

This is a forever moment
We hold in our hands
Yes, we're in a storm
But it's a storm we can stand
As one, as Damien and Junice
And Melissa
Wherever your heart rests
There I will live and be blessed
I've tried to line up the things I
Needed to say but now my feelings just
Tumble from me. I am half foolish,
Half drunk with wanting you
With wanting to take your hand
And leap into the darkness of whatever
Life will bring. Love makes me
Brave and without love I'm made
Nothing.

Aren't you afraid?

Trembling. A bird on a leaf
My hands are numb, my knees weak

With resolution. I am Adam, reeling
From the Garden

Can I be your Eve?
Can you really leave
Yesterday's Damien behind?

I'll never find him again if I search a thousand
    years.

They're getting on the bus, Melissa says.

We're getting on the bus.

Yes. Yes.

JUNICE *with* DAMIEN *and* MELISSA *on* *the* BUS *to* MEMPHIS

As Damien sleeps, I lie with my cheek against
His side. His clothing smells of nervous sweat
The sound of his heart is comforting.
The occasional highway lights flicker through
The half-empty bus. A ghost White woman with
Dark, shiny eyes presses her face against a
   window.
Damien has written a letter to his parents
I imagine him typing, searching for words
Thinking again and again how useless words can be
"I will call you soon," is all that I left for Miss Ruby
What would I add, that it is crying time?
I am crying for Miss Ruby, and vow to find
A place for her, as I will find one for Melissa

In this fearful moment I am crying for Mama
Vowing to forgive her. One day. Some day.

Melissa woke and came from her seat to
Where Damien and I huddled. I smiled
At her and she didn't smile back. But she
Lifted my hand from Damien's shoulder,
Kissed it, and put it carefully back.

I am crying for Damien. He is so beautiful with
His gifts of love, so wise in his reasoning, but I
Wonder if I can be strong enough for him.
And then . . . And then . . . And then I am not
Crying. I am not on a bus but a captain
Battling the tossing sea and I am peering
Straight ahead through the fog and darkness
Knowing that somewhere there is safety,
Somewhere there is a land where we can
Build and plant and grow.
Damien tells me that he has withdrawn
His savings, but worries that it will not
Be enough. I don't answer.

Damien, I am Street, we will make it.

Damien says that we must have a plan to succeed.

Damien, I am Street, I plan to survive.

His voice dropped when he said . . . perhaps . . .
    we should
Marry, his arm pulling me closer.
"We'll see, my love," I answered.
As Damien sleeps, I lie with my cheek against
His side. His clothing smells of nervous sweat
The sound of his heart is comforting.

Also by Walter Dean Myers

FICTION

Autobiography of My Dead Brother
National Book Award Finalist

Crystal

The Dream Bearer

Handbook for Boys: *A Novel*

It Ain't All for Nothin'

Monster
Michael L. Printz Award
Coretta Scott King Author Honor Book
National Book Award Finalist

The Mouse Rap

Patrol: *An American Soldier in Vietnam*
Jane Addams Children's Book Award

The Righteous Revenge of Artemis Bonner

Scorpions
Newbery Honor Book

Shooter

The Story of the Three Kingdoms

NONFICTION

Bad Boy: *A Memoir*

Brown Angels: *An Album of Pictures and Verse*

The Harlem Hellfighters: *When Pride Met Courage*

I've Seen the Promised Land:

    The Life of Dr. Martin Luther King, Jr.

Malcolm X: *A Fire Burning Brightly*

Now Is Your Time!:

    The African-American Struggle for Freedom

    Coretta Scott King Author Award

AWARDS

ALA Margaret A. Edwards Award for lifetime achievement in writing for young adults

ALAN Award for outstanding contribution to the field of young adult literature

Walter Dean Myers is the renowned author of *Autobiography of My Dead Brother*; *Shooter*, a Children's Book Sense Summer Pick; *Monster*, the first winner of the Michael L. Printz Award; *The Dream Bearer*; *Handbook for Boys: A Novel*; *Bad Boy: A Memoir*; and the Newbery Honor Books *Scorpions* and *Somewhere in the Darkness*. He wrote *The Harlem Hellfighters: When Pride Met Courage*; *Patrol: An American Soldier in Vietnam*, illustrated by Ann Grifalconi; *I've Seen the Promised Land: The Life of Dr. Martin Luther King, Jr.* and *Malcolm X: A Fire Burning Brightly*, both illustrated by Leonard Jenkins; and the Caldecott Honor Book *Harlem* and *Blues Journey*, both illustrated by Christopher Myers. He makes frequent appearances with the National Basketball Association's "Read to Achieve" program. Mr. Myers lives with his family in Jersey City, New Jersey.

You can visit him online at www.walterdeanmyersbooks.com.